I

Little Ha-Ha

Christopher Boyce

KISSING DEER PRESS, LLC
California

This book was processed chlorine-free using New Leaf Opaque 70# text and Reincarnation Matte 100# cover, printed using soy-based inks.
4,400 units of this book printed on 100% recycled, 50% post consumer waste paper saved: 5 virgin trees, 440 pounds of solid waste, 632 kilowatt hours of electricity, 484 gallons of water, one cubic yard of land fill space and the equivalent green house gases of 648 miles traveled in the avereage American car. Congratulations!

The Publisher wishes to thank:
R.C.S.
New Leaf Paper
www.newleafpaper.com
Precision Printers
www.precisionprinters.net
Audio International
Ojai, CA

First Kissing Deer Press, LLC Edition
VOLUME ONE

Published by Kissing Deer Press, LLC
1223 Wilshire Blvd., Suite 897, Santa Monica, CA
90403-5400

Manufactured in the United States of America
ISBN: 0-9703704-9-0

0 9 8 7 6 5 4 3 2 1

For "Terri-Walks-with-Flowers"

Little Ha-Ha

In 1864, Little Ha-Ha was nine winters old when he left the comforts of his Oglala tribe by the Greasy Grass Creek in southeastern Montana. He was led by his father, Rain-in-His-Eyes, and a band of agile young warriors, to the sacred hunting grounds of the Shoshone Mountains, five sleeps away, due south.

On the seventh day, Rain-in-His-Eyes pulled a brightly colored arrow from his quiver and launched it airborne from a willow bow he made three summers ago. It only took two arrowheads to bring down a large buck and a doe deer. Little Ha-Ha's father whooped and hollered for joy as he called the warriors in the voice of the coyote and wolf to gather around and share in the bounty.

Four lodges of men (eight) came running over on buckskin-covered feet and riding painted ponies. All but Little Ha-Ha reveled in the good news. The village would eat meat in time for the next full moon.

Rain-in-His-Eyes danced in a circle around the fallen animals, singing and chanting thanks to the Everywhere Spirit for supplying the tribe with a delicious variety of foods; thanks for the skins which would be made into buckskin clothing; and thanks for the hoofs later to be dried and used for the Sun Dance ritual. "Nothing will be wasted from these glorious animals," he said, staring directly at the sky. "Thank you for this blessing, and thank you for allowing Little Ha-Ha to see with his two good eyes and one large brain, the significance of this hunt . . . his first."

Rain then took his son's hand, raised it to the cloudless blue sky and again howled like the wolf to formally end the sacrifice ceremony.

As sacrifice ceremonies go, Rain had done everything properly, just as his father had taught him; and his father's father taught *him;* and his father's, father's, father taught *him;* and his father's, father's, father's, father taught *him*—or so he was told. So that's why Rain was puzzled and somewhat emotionally detached when his son got

sick (in front of all the warriors) on his just-made partially beaded, high-top moccasins.

Attempting to suppress his rage (and embarrassment), Rain lifted his son from the mud of a newly formed puddle, raised the boy's left hand to the sky and placed a large, flat blade in it. "You will come with me to the waters five-horses-wide to clean and prepare these animals for the travois ride home."

Rain looked from the corner of his eye to see if the accompanying warriors had noticed this fine fatherly exchange (they had), then loosened his grip on his son's arm.

Little Ha-Ha shuddered and stammered as little boys do when they can't control their emotions the way they want to.

"What is there to say?" his father yelled. "You will do as you are told. Look at me; I did as I was told—like my father did what *he* was told by *his* father; and *his* father's, father did what *he* was told

4

by *his* father; and *his* father's, father's, father's, father did what *he* was told . . ."

Thinking this was a good time to mosey, Ha-Ha placed a flat foot to the ground and made quick like the antelope. He ran to his pony and rode hard to the hills. He never looked back.

And so, on this windy day, Little Ha-Ha scanned the horizon with his pair of keen eyes and raced to a high butte many breaths-of-a-pony's-run away. He went to a place, a sacred place, where he found a pit dug by a Shoshone eagle catcher who catches eagles there around every time of the hang-nail moon.

Frightened and hungry, Little Ha-Ha lay in the pit and stared at the sky. He tried to think of what had just happened and what it meant for the future of his people—his tribe. He wondered if he could ever look his father in the eyes again, and if he would ever be able to shoot arrows at animals; he wondered many things, but mostly, Little Ha-Ha wanted to have a vision.

So he fasted, went without water,

without food. He stared directly at the bright sky, but did not blink. He placed sharp rocks in his toes to keep from falling asleep. Then he sat on a pile of pebbles and tied white, brown, and red-colored stones behind his ears. He tore off his buckskin shirt and pants—a gift from his grandmother, Holding Needle, for his eighth-winter's birthday. He threw his moccasins to the wind . . . and he waited.

And waited.

For three days he waited for a vision, but no vision came. Not a friendly flyer or a fine four-legged animal visited him; not even the infamous Red-Winged-Neckbiter (the horse fly). Nothing.

Little Ha-Ha began to think that he was not entitled or destined to have a vision; that he was somehow different, an outcast, a sullen anti-social. He wondered if he had what it took to be an elder, a shaman . . . a visionary.

He did.

After three nights and four suns, he returned to the place where his pony stood. He looked to the sky through his wet eyes to see the sun disappearing behind black and gray-colored clouds—clouds not there just moments ago. Together, the clouds and wind were trying to tell him something. Wearing only a buckskin loin cloth and a piece of otter skin to keep his hair in place, Little Ha-Ha grabbed his pony's bridle as if to mount him, but paused. He remained quiet in order to listen—to hear.

He quickly determined that he was too weak to go on. Instead, he dropped the reigns and rested against a tall birch tree. It was there that he fell asleep. And he dreamed.

And dreamed.

He dreamed a great vision and spoke out loud as if addressing the Everywhere Spirit: "I am on the backbone of the world (the Shoshone Mountains); I see a woman—I mean a girl—born during the season when the leaves return (spring), seven times ago. She has a name about her . . . Teri . . . with two R's . . . Terri-Walks-with-Flowers. That is the name given to her by her blessed mother and father.

"She walks in a happy circle with a great white buffalo. She comes from a place near the headwaters of the Sweetwater River. Tall, blond sweet grass grows in abundance according to the will of the sun. She is many gifted. She sings in the voice of the chickadee and can talk with the owls. All animals of the sky and the good and beautiful Earth welcomed her to the Nation on the hour of her birth.

"I see when she was born, a white buffalo roamed into her tipi. Everyone in the village was happy—this was a good sign. This was a sign from the Great Spirit. Make no mistake. I see for three full moons, the white Buffalo refused to leave the tipi without the presence of the girl. This caused a great stink to the general area. When the neighbors thought about complaining, they decided not to; they cleansed their minds of these thoughts when the buffalo refused to budge. It was okay, soon all was forgiven, but the fact remained—a white buffalo

was living in a tipi twenty-eight hands tall (15'6"), just two flaps away (practically next door) . . . and he wouldn't go anywhere without Terri-Walks-with-Flowers."

By this time, Little Ha-Ha's pony was getting tired of standing and decided to lay down next to the boy who trained him, although the pony could not fathom why he was dressed so funny and talking to the air.

It did not matter.

The pony loved the boy. Ha-Ha was an excellent rider. He never, never, ever kicked his heels into his ribs to make him "go" and he never forgot (not even once) to feed him sweet and sour apples after long days of jumping coulees and riding through tall grass, thistle weeds, and sage brush.

Anyhow, Little Ha-Ha was still talking: "Seven seasons of full leaves pass and beauty and abundance is heaped on the village where the girl and the buffalo reside. Everybody has many gifts of food. The children, the men, the women, the elders, and the visionaries are all well dressed and walk with a spring in their step. Everyone says, 'How-How-Ha!' in greeting when they show their high-cheek-boned faces in the morning. The time is good. The trout in the river have made fat; they are beautiful to look at, but more fun to eat; they no longer play hide-and-go-seek, they cooperate to get caught by saying, 'Look here! Look at my tasty meat!'

"Everyone has teeth and can partake in the bounty of the plentiful, gracious Earth. The girl and the buffalo direct the sweet and fertile water from the creek to feed and nourish the tall grass and wildflowers. She grows squash, corn, pumpkins, turnips, and wild iris; acorns, pine nuts, and bitterroot grow side-by-side next to wild onion, cucumber, zucchini, and five different types of lettuce—I see she makes a wonderful salad."

Without knowing why, Ha-Ha wiped saliva from the corner of his mouth before continuing with his dream.

"After vegetable supper, she gathers the men and women together for more treats, more gifts. Buffalo berries, chokecherries, elderberries, wild plums, cactus buds, and crab apples, are gathered together in a nifty dough of her design and baked under hot rocks for the length of time it takes for Long Hair (General Custer) to make a mistake, that's all—not long."

Once again, Ha-Ha pulled at his wet lips as his stomach made the sound of a mountain lion who has been trapped in the trees too long.

"I see that while the pie is being born, the people are singing and dancing. They want to keep the secret of the girl and the buffalo in the village—their village; they do not want to share for reasons unclear to me—but the girl has different plans, I think . . . yes, yes, she wants to take the white buffalo with her to lands previously unseen to her waking eyes. . . ."

Ha-Ha's pony flicked his tail over the boy's face to distract the Red-Winged-Neckbiter and other undesirables from interrupting the vision. However, the pony grew impatient wondering when it will all be over so he could put his nose where it does not belong.

The boy continued: "But she is not without needs, I see; she is missing something for sure; what it is, I cannot exactly tell."

Ha-Ha's pony continued to provide a clear vision for the boy of many words, but quietly thought in his big pony brain: "There is a fine filly of a mare with long blonde hair and white spots on her shoulders; she is over by Murky Creek and I would like to see her ASAP. I would like the boy to be done now."

But he wasn't.

"Ah. Ah. I see. I see. She wants to go on a moccasin telegraph—but she has no moccasins. She must leave because she has gifts and visions too large to contain in one village alone. I also see her pie of darkening berries is nearly done. I wish I could taste it; I'm quite hungry . . . mmmmmmm—anyway, she needs beaded-buckskin mocs to walk with

honor and tell her visions. Her village, thanks to her, is endowed with many talents; many gifted and blessed people live there, however, a seamstress is nowhere to be found."

Off in the near distance, a grouping of small birds jumped from their perch of a white-bark pine. Ha-ha was startled, then awakened by the soft pitter-patter of approaching footsteps.

Rain-in-His-Eyes stood over his son's body, blocking the sun's rays from the child's vision-colored face.

"You have been gone for three sleeps and four suns without telling anyone. Your mother urged me in no uncertain language to look for you until you have been found."

"I have been found; I have been found," interjected Ha-Ha, as he wiped his wet, swollen eyes.

"You would not have been found were it not for my superior hunting eyes and the concern of your mother and her mother; and her mother's, mother; and her mother's, mother's, mother; and come to think of it, her mother's, mother's, mother's, mother's, mother . . ."

And so on.

Ha-Ha recognized his father's anger, though he was not frightened by it. He no longer had any fear.

So, as his father continued to berate him, the boy looked above and beyond the father to a place where good things come from—the sky—and saw a pair of multi-colored, beaded moccasins, size five, floating around the sun in a clockwise fashion.

He did not tell his father of the vision, but remained silent. The significance had not eluded him. Ha-Ha knew he could not shuck the weight of what just happened.

He would help lead his people to light and greatness; but mostly, he would hold and cherish the vision forever. *Visions and dreams are precious things*, he thought to himself. *I will hold them in the place where my heart is kept . . . always, forever.*

When Rain-in-His-Eyes brought

Ha-Ha back to the village, he told the boy in no uncertain terms that he was grassed (grounded) and not to leave the entrance flap of the tipi.

Later that night, when he thought his son was asleep, Rain spoke to his wife, She-Has-Two-Bears, from a place where there was much pain . . . his head.

"Our son made a mockery of the hunting party; he embarrassed me, my father, his father—"

"Stop with the family stuff," said Two-Bears, rolling her eyes to the smoke hole in the tipi.

"The boy really lived up to his name I tell you," resumed Rain. "The hunting party ha-ha'd all the way through Wyoming Territory, all the way to Greasy Grass, and they are still laughing as I speak. What kind of a boy is he who doesn't like to hunt? I liked to hunt when I was a boy; as a father I like to hunt; my father liked to hunt . . . come to think of it, his father—"

"I will be a happy Indian if you never

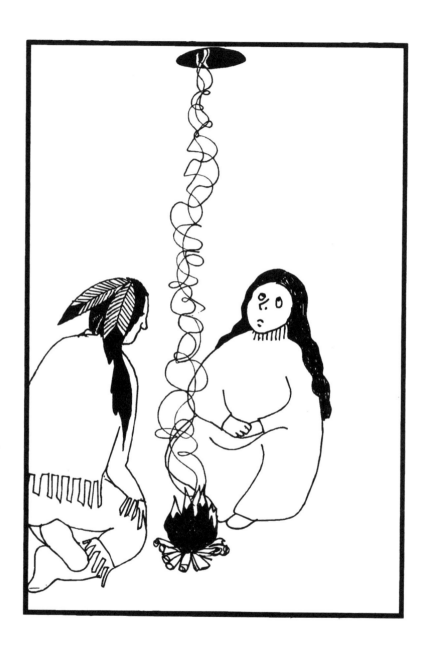

use those words again. Do you wish to make me happy?" asked Two-Bears.

"Why yes, of course; it is of the most importance, or so I'm told. But woman, I'll tell you the thing that would make *me* happy. I want to sell Little Ha-Ha to the Flatheads. I figure we could get a good rate. . . ."

Two-Bears jumped to her feet and placed her fists on her hips. "No. No way," she said.

"Okay, then I will sell him to the Blackfeet."

"You will not!" glowered Two-Bears.

"Ahhhhhh . . . trade. I'll trade with the Rocky Boys, say, for twelve horses, six blankets, and some repeating rifles—Winchesters, preferably."

She-Has-Two-Bears put her foot down, like a horse does when he wants oats instead of alfalfa. "Little Ha-Ha is not for sale. He is not for trade. Not to the Cheyenne, the Rocky Boys, or the Blackfeet—not to anyone, anywhere, at anytime."

"Woman, you would make a fine

horse trader. You hold firm. That's good. But what about the cavalry? I hear they are looking for a few good Indian scouts. We could be in bacon 'till the moon of shedding ponies (July)."

Ha-Ha, having heard his father's wishes, slowly crawled from his sleeping area to the tipi of his grandmother, Holding Needle. In the comfort of his grandmother's arms, Ha-Ha asked the old woman to grant him one wish. He asked, without telling her why, for her to assemble the finest pair of beaded moccasins known to Indian and non-Indian alike. He asked that she stitch in whistle bone and golden hops where the laces go. Fine sunflowers should be on the bumps of each ankle; on top of the toes, a proud white buffalo should appear like he is floating in air, his hoofs not touching the ground. The mocs should have extra padding in the heel, so the wearer would not say hello to shin splints. And finally, he requested, they must be done by two hours before the

next sun disappears behind the mountains (5:36 P.M.).

His grandmother nodded once and raised a calloused palm to her grandson. Knowing this to mean "be gone now," Ha-Ha did so, crawled back to his parents' tipi, slipped into the warmth of his buffalo blanket and promptly fell asleep.

Outside, a full moon lit up an ignorant black night. And under it all, many sleeps away, Terri-Walks-with-Flowers (covered by a flannel blanket), stared into the eyes of her very alive, very white buffalo, and prayed quietly to the Great Spirit. Her soul was growing impatient.

The next day, the sun was between Yellow-Cow's tipi and Young-Man-Afraid-of-the-Dark-Afraid-of-the-Horses-Afraid-of-the-Trout's tipi (about twelve noon), when Ha-Ha's village rose to eat their breakfast of dried roots and insects sprinkled with a bit of brown sugar from the Sandwich Islands (Hawaii).

Anyway, by this time Ha-Ha was wide awake and active; he already shook hands with and smiled at almost everyone in the village before helping his great aunt prepare a food tray for a shaman who was not feeling well. He built a mountain out of parsley and spinach, accented with apples and acorns. He did all these things well so he would not be late for what was soon to unfold.

Ha-Ha could barely contain his excitement as he opened the flap of his grandmother's tipi. Inside, the old and wise woman pulled the last stitch from the magic moccasins before exclaiming, "Oooooh. Ya! Ya! Ha!" She was very happy.

Ha-Ha smiled at his grandmother. The moccasins were stunning; what's more, he knew they would do the trick. What he did not know, however, was how to bring the moccasins to the girl or the girl to the moccasins. He wondered if he needed another vision. But when he looked at the intricate sweet grass and herb detail, he realized, at that moment, what he must do.

At that exact same time, that exact moment, many sleeps away, Terri-Walks-with-Flowers had an epiphany not too different from Little Ha-Ha's. She began to cry, for reasons unbeknownst to her and without warning she cried. (Upon her birth, the Great Spirit had sprinkled angels in her eyes and colored her cheekbones with freckles, just for moments like this.) Then, in a corner of her parents' tipi, the white buffalo, its head on low, its tail on high, walked in a tight, clockwise circle. In the center of the circle, a radiant, warming sun lay on the ground.

Rays of soothing, fragmented, and splintered light stretched in all directions. The light grew and grew; nothing got in its way. It inched slowly at first, out of the tipi to the area where the gifts grow (the garden).

Once it touched the sweet grass, it immediately grew to the height of a pony's hip (about 4'9" tall). The light transcended

through the legs of everyone in the village—through children who ran to chase it, through the elders and visionaries who bent to touch it—the light knew no boundaries. It shot to the banks of the Sweetwater River, over the crested high buttes, to fields of lupine, Indian paintbrush, and wild sunflowers.

As if in a trance, Terri followed the light heading north; she did not ask why, she just walked—barefoot. The buffalo did the same, only he lagged slightly behind because he was still walking like this, so it took a while.

Anyway, by this time, Ha-Ha held the magic moccasins in his right hand while clamoring over hills and valleys to his intended emotional destination. He did not know where his heart or his mind were leading him. He did not care; he didn't want to know.

What he did know, however, was that every animal from the village began to follow him on his journey. In fact, all of the animals from the surrounding forests, creeks and rivers along the way followed too. (If you are having trouble picturing this, just imagine a trout jumping out of the water—the way trout do—and landing, somehow, on the back of a sturdy animal vehicle; say a doe, a female deer; or a badger; or a big horn sheep). None of the animals really cared since they were all going to the same place and would probably return along the same or similar route, so no living creature would get displaced from the homes they loved so very much. The whole incident worked like greased lightning and was brilliant to watch. It made you cry.

Anyhow, by this time, Terri-Walks-with-Flowers was really living up to her name on account she walked holding flowers, but she continued to cry. So don't think that just because a person is holding flowers when he or she is walking, that it makes them immune from feeling melancholy, because it doesn't. In fact, in her case it probably exacerbated the situation, though she had no way of knowing; the animals knew, as animals do, but they did not tell her. Not because they were being difficult, but because they knew it was always darkest before the storm and that this too shall pass. She should take one day at a time because there is no gain without pain and it should be the Great Spirit's will, not your own. The animals knew that—but you can't tell another person those things; one has to figure them out oneself. So there.

So anyhow, the animals really helped—a lot more than they are given credit for these days, which is a shame because they are disappearing, one-by-one, as we speak. But we know that. Terri knew that too, which could account for some of her tears, though there is no way of knowing for sure, so she just walked on.

She walked for three sleeps without sleeping and witnessed the sunrise from where the sun rises (the east). She went without food and water (though it was all around her) and she didn't stop walking

until she reached the Backbone of the World.

She sat under a tall birch tree, reclining her legs on the warm ground before her. The white buffalo circled once around Terri and sat down. He instructed the other animals to do the same, but over yonder; he didn't want to be crowded, he said. So they did. And all the animals shared the same food and drank from the same water without complaining—not even once. The trout were deposited in a pond with a cascading waterfall that brought many delicious worms, insects, and things to replenish their tummies. They were happy beyond compare.

Right around this time, Little Ha-Ha was making his way to the same mountain, in the very same way, with the same amount of animals in tow (minus one white buffalo).

A magpie flew in a circular manner around Ha-Ha's head and seemed to point a wing to the top of the mountain, about fifty-six breaths-of-a-running-horse away

(110 yards). "Thank you," said Little Ha-Ha, focusing his eyes and countenance to the lone tree on top of the mountain.

He walked on.

A beaming smile graced his baby teeth as he stared in wide-eyed wonder at the blessed flower child lying in a stupendous array of golden grass, peonies, dahlias, daisies, daffodils, and lady slippers.

The white buffalo told the animals in Ha-Ha's party to go and rest with the others. They did so on account that all of them were fluent in buffalo and didn't question his authority.

Ha-Ha stopped about four lengths of a pony (twenty-six feet) from the girl and the buffalo.

Terri looked over her shoulder. "Come over," she said, in a lenient manner all her own. "Come over."

And he did.

"I have seen your face before on a mountain—this mountain—The Backbone of the World," said Little Ha-Ha. "I have

seen the gifts you design and give freely of to anybody in need. I have seen the salad you make, but have wondered just what kind of dressing you sprinkle on top. I bet it is complementary to the taste buds in the mouth and leaves them wanting more. I have seen the glory of the union in your tribe and often wonder—as little boys do—if other tribes in the Nation can possess such clarity. You are blessed, not to mention insightful and honest—the highest quality that a human being of the Nation can hope for. You have all these things and more, but you still lack a decent pair of moccasins."

Ha-Ha darted a quick tongue over his lips before looking at the girl, the buffalo, then back to the girl.

"I have seen you . . . in my mind . . . in my heart . . . running a moccasin telegraph while that buffalo next to you issues smoke signals to a land beautiful and far away. You have much work to do, that is certain; that you are wise beyond the years of your age is also a fact."

By this time, the buffalo thought he

had heard all the niceties he could fathom, so he rolled his great buffalo eyes, indicating to the boy to make his point and cut to the chase.

It did not go unnoticed.

"Anyway," said Little Ha-Ha, "you and I are leaving this world today for the real world beyond this one. We will both walk on a path we do not know. We go with protection from the Great Spirit. Fortitude, guidance, and light will be the focus given to us from the Everywhere Spirit," Ha-Ha said, as he placed the palm of his hand over his rapidly beating heart.

He stepped closer to the girl.

"But before we go," he said, "I must give you these." Little Ha-Ha extended the supple moccasins to Terri.

She smiled as she slipped them on. *A perfect size five*, she thought. *And some extra padding in the heel—nice touch.* She wouldn't be saying hello to shin splints, bunions or corns. She grinned at the sunflowers and touched the whistle bone, sweet grass, and herb detail implemented tastefully from heel to toe. Even the

buffalo winked his approval when he saw his likeness stitched on top of the toes.

No symbol had been overlooked, none left out. They were complete. And now, so too were the boy, Little Ha-Ha and the girl, Terri-Walks-with-Flowers.

"Come over. Sit," said Terri, patting the earth. "We must kiss to seal the understanding given to us by the Spirits. Then we have to sleep under a dream-filled sky so we can dance and skip on clouds white like snow. We must do so now," requested the girl, wiping a smooth hand over a moist and freckled cheek.

And so they did. And the animals did too. And all enjoyed the boon of sleep so tender, so heartfelt . . . it made them all cry.

You may contact the author at:
www.littlehaha.com